A Hundred Camels
in the Courtyard

PAUL BOWLES

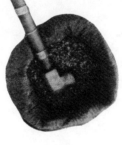

CITY LIGHTS BOOKS
San Francisco

A HUNDRED CAMELS IN THE COURTYARD
Copyright ©1962, 1981, 1986 by Paul Bowles
All rights reserved
Published 1962. Second Edition 1986
Printed in the United States of America

Cover photograph by Paul Bowles

Photograph of Paul Bowles by Allen Ginsberg
courtesy of Allen Ginsberg

Zemmour *Hanbel* (19th century)
courtesy of Musée Dar Jamai, Meknes

Design by Bob Sharrard & Kim McCloud
Typography by Francisco de Oliveira Mattos
& Lorry Fleming, Re/Search

Some of these stories appeared originally in
The London Magazine, Big Table, and *Encounter.*
"Preface" appeared originally in the phonodisc
Paul Bowles Reads A Hundred Camels (Cadmus Editions, 1981),
reprinted by permission.

ISBN 0-87286-002-7

CITY LIGHTS BOOKS are edited by Lawrence Ferlinghetti
& Nancy J. Peters and published at the City Lights Bookstore,
261 Columbus Avenue, San Francisco, California 94133.

CONTENTS

A pipe of kif before breakfast gives a man the strength of a hundred camels in the courtyard.

— NCHAIOUI PROVERB

PREFACE

Moroccan kif-smokers like to speak of "two worlds", the one ruled by inexorable natural laws, and the other, the kif world, in which each person perceives "reality" according to the projections of his own essence, the state of consciousness in which the elements of the physical universe are automatically rearranged by cannabis to suit the requirements of the individual. These distorted variations in themselves generally are of scant interest to anyone but the subject at the time he is experiencing them. An intelligent smoker, nevertheless, can aid in directing the process of deformation in such a way that the results will have value to him in his daily life. If he has faith in the accuracy of his interpretations, he will accept them as decisive, and use them to determine a subsequent plan of action. Thus, for a dedicated smoker, the passage to the "other world" is often a pilgrimage undertaken for the express purpose of oracular consultation.

In 1960 I began to experiment with the idea of constructing stories whose subject matter would consist of disparate elements and unrelated characters taken directly from life and fitted together as in a mosaic. The problem was to create a story line which would make each arbitrarily chosen episode compatable with the others, to make each one lead to the next with a semblance of naturalness. I believed that through the intermediary of kif the barriers separating the unrelated elements might be destroyed, and the disconnected episodes forced into a symbiotic relationship. I listed a group of incidents and situations I had either witnessed or heard about that year.

A. had an old grudge against B. When B. was made a policeman, A. sent money to him, seeing to it that B.'s superior was made aware of the gift. B. was reprimanded and given a post in the Sahara.

C. acquired an old pair of shoes from D. When he had them resoled he discovered that he could no longer get them on. As a result he quarreled with D.

In another personal feud, E. consulted with a witch to help him deal with his enemy F.

Finding his kitten dead with a needle in its stomach, G. decided that it had been killed because he had named it Mimí.

H. slipped a ring over the head of a stray bird, and the bird flew away with it.

I. although brought up as a Jilali, hated and feared the Jilali.

J. ate so many cactus fruit that the peelings covered his gun and he was unable to find it.

K. frightened a Jewish woman by leaving the ingredients of magic on her doorstep.

This constituted the bulk of the factual material I gave myself to work with. To get three stories out of it, I combined A., B., G. and K. (for *A Friend of the World*); and C., D., and H. (for *The Story of Lahcen and Idir*; and E., F., I. and J. (for *The Wind at Beni Midar*). No one of the actual situations had anything to do with kif, but by providing kif-directed motivations I was able to use cannabis both as solvent and solder in the construction.

He of the Assembly has no factual anchors apart from three hermetic statements made to me that year by a kif-smoker in Marrakech: "The eye wants to sleep, but the head is no mattress," "The earth trembles and the sky is afraid, and the two eyes are not brothers," and "A pipe of kif before breakfast gives a man the strength of a hundred camels in the courtyard." He uttered these apocalyptic sentences, but steadfastly refused to shed any light on their meanings or possible applications. This impelled me to invent a story about him in which he would furnish the meanings. Here the content of each paragraph is determined by its point of view. There are seven paragraphs, arranged in a simple pattern: imagine the cross-section of a pyramidal structure of four steps, where steps 1 and 7 are at the same level, likewise 2 and 6, and 3 and 5, with 4 at the top. In paragraphs 1 and 7 He of the Assembly and Ben Tajah are seen together. 2 and 6 are seen by Ben Tajah, and 3 and 5 by He of the Assembly, and 4 consists of He of the Assembly's interior monologue.

A FRIEND OF THE WORLD

A FRIEND OF THE WORLD

Salam rented two rooms and a kitchen on the second floor of a Jewish house at the edge of the town. He had decided to live with the Jews because he had already lived with Christians and found them all right. He trusted them a little more than he did other Moslems, who were like him and said: "No Moslem can be trusted." Moslems are the only true people, the only people you can understand. But because you do understand them, you do not trust them. Salam did not trust the Jews completely, either, but he liked living with them because they paid no attention to him. It had no importance if they talked about him among themselves, and they never would talk about him to Moslems. If he had a sister who lived here and there, getting what money she could from whatever man she found, because she had to eat, that was all right, and the Jews did not point at her when she came to visit him. If he did not get married, but lived instead with his brother and spent his time smoking kif and laughing, if he got his money by going to Tangier once a month and sleeping for a week with old English and American ladies who drank too much whiskey, they did not care. He was a Moslem. Had he been rich he would have lived in the Spanish end of the town in a villa with concrete benches in the garden and a big round light in the ceiling of the *sala*, with many pieces of glass hanging down from it. He was poor and he lived with the Jews. To get to his house he had to go to the end of the Medina, cross an open space where the trees had all been cut down, go along the street where the warehouses had been abandoned by the Spanish when they left, and into a newer, dirtier street that led to the main highway. Halfway down was the entrance to the alley where he and his brother and fourteen Jewish families lived. There were the remains of narrow sidewalks along the edges of the wide gutter, full of mounds of rotten watermelon-rind and piles of broken bricks. The small children played here all day. When he was in a hurry he had to be careful not to step on them as they waded in the little puddles of dishwater and urine there were in front of all the doors. If they had been Moslem children he would have spoken to them, but since they were Jews he did not see them as children at all, but merely as nuisances in his way, like cactuses that had to be stepped over carefully because there was no way of going around them. Although he had lived here for almost two years, he did not know the names of any of the Jews. For him they had no names. When he came home and found his door locked, because his brother had gone out and taken both keys with him, he went into any house where the door was open and dropped his bundles on the floor, saying: "I'll be back in a little while." He knew they would not touch his property. The Jews were neither friendly nor unfriendly. They too, if they had had money, would have been living in the Spanish end of the town. It made the alley seem less like a Mellah, where only Jews live, to have two Moslems staying among them.

A Friend of the World

Salam had the best house in the alley. It was at the end, and its windows gave onto a wilderness of fig trees and canebrake where squatters had built huts out of thatch and hammered pieces of tin. On the hot nights (for the town was in a plain and the heat stayed in the streets long after the sun had gone) his rooms had a breeze from the south that blew through and out onto the terrace. He was happy with his house and with the life that he and his brother had in it. "I'm a friend of the world," he would say. "A clean heart is better than everything."

One day he came home and found a small kitten sitting on the terrace. When it saw him it ran to him and purred. He unlocked the door into the kitchen and it went inside. After he had washed his hands and feet in the kitchen he went into his room. The kitten was lying on the mattress, still purring. "Mimí," he said to it. He gave it some bread. While it ate the bread it did not stop purring. Bou Ralem came home. He had been drinking beer with some friends in the Café Granada. At first he did not understand why Salam had let the kitten stay. "It's too young to be worth anything," he said. "If it saw a rat it would run and hide." But when the kitten lay in his lap and played with him he liked it. "Its name is Mimí," Salam told him. Nights it slept on the mattress with Salam near his feet. It learned to go down into the alley to relieve itself in the dirt there. The children sometimes tried to catch it, but it ran faster than they did and got to the steps before them, and they did not dare follow it upstairs.

During Ramadan, when they stayed up all night, they moved the mats and cushions and mattresses out onto the terrace and lived out there, talking and laughing until the daylight came. They smoked more kif than usual, and invited their friends home at two in the morning for dinner. Because they were living outside and the kitten could hear them from the alley, it grew bolder and began to visit the canebrake behind the house. It could run very fast, and even if a dog chased it, it could get to the stairs in time. When Salam missed it he would stand up and call to it over the railing, on one side down the alley and on the other over the trees and the roofs of the shacks. Sometimes when he was calling into the alley a Jewish woman would run out of one of the doors and look at him. He noticed that it was always the same woman. She would put one hand above her eyes and stare up at him, and then she would put both hands on her hips and frown. "A crazy woman," he thought, and paid no attention to her. One day while he was calling the kitten, the woman shouted up to him in Spanish. Her voice sounded very angry. "*Oyé!*" she cried, shaking her arm in the air, "why are you calling the name of my daughter?"

Salam kept calling: "Mimí! *Agi! Agiagi,* Mimí!"

The woman moved closer to the steps. She put both hands above her eyes, but the sun was behind Salam, so that she could not see him very well. "You want to insult people?" she screamed. "I understand your game. You make fun of me and my daughter."

Salam laughed. He put the end of his forefinger to the side of his head and made circles with it. "I'm calling my cat. Who's your daughter?"

"And your cat is called Mimí because you knew my little girl's name was Mimí. Why don't you behave like civilized people?"

18

Salam laughed again and went inside. He did not think of the woman again. Not many days after that the kitten disappeared, and no matter how much he called, it did not come back. He and Bou Ralem went out that night and searched for it in the canebrake. The moon was bright, and they found it lying dead, and carried it back to the house to look at it. Someone had given it a pellet of bread with a needle inside. Salam sat slowly on the mattress. "The Yehoudía," he said.

"You don't know who did it," Bou Ralem told him.

"It was the Yehoudía. Throw me the *mottoui*." And he began to smoke kif, one pipe after another. Bou Ralem understood that Salam was looking for an answer, and he did not talk. After a while he saw that the time had come to turn off the electricity and light the candle. When he had done this, Salam lay back quietly on the mattress and listened to the dogs barking outside. Now and then he sat up and filled his *sebsi*. Once he passed it to Bou Ralem, and lay back down on the cushions smiling. He had an idea of what he would do. When they went to bed he said to Bou Ralem: "She's one mother who's going to wet her pants."

The next day he got up early and went to the market. In a little stall there he bought several things: a crow's wing, a hundred grams of *jduq jmel* seeds, powdered porcupine quills, some honey, a pressed lizard, and a quarter kilo of *fasoukh*. When he had finished paying for all this he turned away as if he were going to leave the stall, then he said: "*Khaï*, give me another fifty grams of *jduq jmel*." When the man had weighed the seeds out and put them into a paper and folded it up, he paid him and carried the paper in his

left hand as he went on his way home. In the alley the
children were throwing clots of mud at one another. They
stopped while he went by. The women sat in the doorways
with their shawls over their heads. As he passed before the
house of the woman who had killed Mimí he let go of the
package of *jduq jmel* seeds. Then he went upstairs onto his
terrace, walked to the door, and pounded on it. No one
answered. He stood in the middle of the terrace where everyone could see him, rubbing his hand over his chin. A
minute later he climbed to the terrace next to his and
knocked on that door. He handed his parcel to the woman
who came to open. "I left my keys in the market," he told
her. "I'll be right back." He ran downstairs, through the
alley, and up the street.

Behind the Gailan Garage Bou Ralem was standing.
When Salam passed him, he nodded his head once and went
along without stopping. Bou Ralem began to walk in the
other direction, back to the house. As he opened the gate
onto the terrace, the woman from next door called to him.
"Haven't you seen your brother? He left his keys in the
market." "No," Bou Ralem said, and went in, leaving the
door open. He sat down and smoked a cigarette while he
waited. In a little while the talking in the alley below
sounded louder. He stood up and went to the door to listen.
A woman was crying: "It's *jduq jmel*! Mimí had it in her
hand!" Soon there were many more voices, and the woman
from the next terrace ran downstairs in her bathrobe, carrying a parcel. "That's it," Bou Ralem said to himself. When
she arrived the shouting grew louder. He listened for a time,
smiling. He went out and ran downstairs. They were all in

the alley outside the woman's door, and the little girl was inside the house, screaming. Without looking toward them he ran by on the far side of the alley.

Salam was inside the café, drinking a glass of tea. "Sit down," he told Bou Ralem. "I'm not going to get Fatma Daifa before eleven." He ordered his brother a tea. "Were they making a lot of noise?" he asked him. Bou Ralem nodded his head. Salam smiled. "I'd like to hear them," he said. "You'll hear them," Bou Ralem told him. "They're not going to stop."

At eleven o'clock they left the café and went through the back passages of the Medina to Fatma Daifa's house. She was the sister of their mother's mother, and thus not of their family, so that they did not feel it was shameful to use her in the game. She was waiting for them at the door, and together they went back to Salam's house.

The old woman went into the alley ahead of Salam and Bou Ralem, and walked straight to the door where all the women were gathered. She held her *haïk* tightly around her head so that no part of her face showed, except one eye. She pushed against the Jewish women and held out one hand. "Give me my things," she told them. She did not bother to speak Spanish with them because she knew they understood Arabic. "You have my things." They did have them and they were still looking at them, but then they turned to look at her. She seized all the packages and put them into her *kouffa* quickly. "No shame!" she shouted at the women. "Go and look after your children." She pushed the other way and went back into the alley where Salam and Bou Ralem stood waiting. The three went upstairs and into

21

Salam's house,and they shut the door. They had lunch there
and stayed all day, talking and laughing. When everyone
had gone to bed, Salam took Fatma Daifa home.

The next day the Jews all stared at them when they
went out, but no one said anything to them. The woman
Salam had wanted to frighten did not come to her door at
all, and the little girl was not in the alley playing with the
other children. It was clear that the Jews thought Fatma
Daifa had put a spell on the child. They would not have
believed Salam and Bou Ralem alone could do such a thing,
but they knew a Moslem woman had the power. The two
brothers were very much pleased with the joke. It is forbid-
den to practice magic, but the old woman was their witness
that they had not done such a thing. She had taken home all
the packages just as they had been when she had snatched
them away from the Jewish women, and she had promised
to keep them that way, so that in case of trouble she could
prove that nothing had been used.

The Jewish woman went to the *comisaría* to complain.
She found a young policeman sitting at his desk listening to
a small radio he had in his hand, and she began to tell him
that the Moslems in her *haouma* had bought charms to use
against her daughter. The policeman did not like her, partly
because she was Jewish and spoke Spanish instead of
Arabic, and partly because he did not approve of people
who believed in magic, but he listened politely until she
said: "That Moslem is a *sinvergüenza*." She tried to go on to
say that there were many very good Moslems, but he did not
like her words. He frowned at the woman and said: "Why do
you say all this? What makes you think they put a spell on

your little girl?" She told him how the three had shut themselves in all day with the packages of bad things from the market. The policeman looked at her in surprise. "And for a dead lizard you came all the way here?" he laughed. He sent her away and went on listening to his radio.

The people in the alley still did not speak to Salam and Bou Ralem, and the little girl did not come out to play in the mud with the others. When the woman went to the market she took her with her. "Hold on to my skirt," she would tell her. But one day in front of the service station the child let go of the woman's skirt for a minute. When she ran to catch up with her mother, she fell and her knee hit a broken bottle. The woman saw the blood and began to scream. People stopped walking. In a few minutes a Jew came by and helped the woman carry the child to a pharmacy. They bandaged the little girl's knee and the woman took her home. Then she went back to the pharmacy to get her baskets, but on the way she stopped at the police station. She found the same policeman sitting at his desk.

"If you want to see the proof of what I told you, come and look at my little girl now," she told him. "Again?" said the policeman. He was not friendly with her, but he took her name and address, and later that day on his way home he called at her house. He looked at the little girl's knee and tickled her ribs so that she laughed. "All children fall down," he said. "But who is this Moslem? Where does he live?" The mother showed him the stairs at the end of the alley. He did not intend to speak with Salam, but he wanted to finish with the woman once and for all. He went out into the alley, and saw that the woman was watching him from

23

the door, so he walked slowly to the foot of the stairs. When he had decided she was no longer looking, he started to go. At that moment he heard a voice behind him. He turned and saw Salam standing above him on the terrace. He did not much like his face, and he told himself that if ever he saw him in the street he would have a few words with him.

One morning Salam went early to the market to get fresh kif. When he found it he bought three hundred francs' worth. As he went out through the gates into the street the policeman, who was waiting for him, stopped him. "I want to speak with you," he told him. Salam stretched his fingers tightly around the kif in his pocket. "Is everything all right?" said the policeman. "Everything is fine," Salam replied. "No trouble?" the policeman insisted, looking at him as if he knew what Salam had just bought. Salam answered: "No trouble." The policeman said: "See that it stays like that." Salam was angry at being spoken to in this way for no reason, but with the kif in his pocket he could only be thankful he was not being searched. "I'm a friend of the world," he said, trying to smile. The policeman did not answer, and turned away.

"A very bad thing," thought Salam as he hurried home with the kif. No policeman had bothered him before this. When he reached his room he wondered if he should hide the package under a tile in the floor, but he decided that if he did that, he himself would be living like a Jew, who each time there is a knock at the door ducks his head and trembles. He spread the kif out on the table defiantly and left it there. During the afternoon he and Bou Ralem cut it. He did not mention the policeman, but he was thinking of him all

24

the time they were working. When the sun had gone down behind the plain and the soft breeze began to come in through the windows he took off his shirt and lay back on the pillows to smoke. Bou Ralem filled his *mottoui* with the fresh kif and went out to a café. "I'm staying here," said Salam.

He smoked for an hour or more. It was a hot night. The dogs had begun to bark in the canebrake. A woman and a man in one of the huts below were cursing one another. Sometimes the woman stopped shouting and merely screamed. The sound bothered Salam. He could not be happy. He got up and dressed, took his *sebsi* and his *mottoui*, and went out. Instead of turning toward the town when he left the alley, he walked toward the highway. He wanted to sit in a quiet place in order to find out what to do. If the policeman had not suspected him, he would not have stopped him. Since he had stopped him once, he might do it again, and the next time he might search him. "That's not freedom", he said to himself. A few cars went by. Their headlights made the tree-trunks yellow as they passed. After each car had gone, there was only the blue light of the moon and the sky. When he got to the bridge over the river, he climbed down a bank under the girders, and went along a path to a rock that hung out high above the water. There he sat and looked over the edge at the deep muddy river that was moving below in the moonlight. He felt the kif in his head, and he knew he was going to make it work for him.

He put the plan together slowly. It was going to cost a thousand francs, but he had that, and he was willing to spend it. After six pipes, when he had everything arranged in his mind, he stuffed his *sebsi* into his pocket, jumped up, and climbed the path to the highway. He walked back to the town quickly, going into the Medina by a dirt road where the houses had gardens, and where behind the walls all along the way there were dogs barking at the moon. Not many people walked at night in this part of town. He went to the house of his cousin Abdallah, who was married to a woman from Sidi Kacem. The house was never empty. Two or three of her brothers were always there with their families. Salam spoke privately with Abdallah in the street outside the door, asking for one of the brothers whose face was not known in the town. Abdallah went in and quickly came out again with someone. The man had a beard, wore a country *djellaba*, and carried his shoes in his hand. They spoke together for a few minutes. "Go with him," said Abdallah, when they had finished talking. Salam and the bearded man said goodnight and went away.

At Salam's house that night the man slept on a mat in the kitchen. When morning came, they washed and had coffee and pastries. While they were eating Salam took out his thousand-franc note and put it into an envelope. On the outside of it Bou Ralem had printed the word GRACIAS in pencil. Soon Salam and the man from the country got up and went out through the town until they came to a side street opposite the back entrance of the police station. There they stood against the wall and talked. "You don't know his name," said the man. "We don't have to," Salam told him. "When he comes out and gets into one of the cars and drives away, you run over to the office and give them the envelope, and say you tried to catch him before he left." He waved the envelope in his hand. "Ask them to give this to him when he comes back. They'll take it."

"He may walk," said the man. "Then what will I do?"

"The police never walk," Salam said. "You'll see. Then you run out again. This street is the best one. Keep going, that's all. I won't be here. I'll see you at Abdallah's."

They waited a long time. The sun grew hotter and they moved into the shade of a fig tree, always watching the door of the *comisaría* from where they stood. Several policemen came out, and for each one the man from the country was ready to run, but Salam held on to him and said: "No, no, no!" When the policeman they were waiting for finally did stand in the doorway, Salam drew in his breath and whispered: "There he is. Wait till he drives off, then run." He turned away and walked very fast down the street into the Medina.

When the man from the country had explained clearly who the envelope was for, he handed it to the policeman at the desk, said: "Thank you," and ran out quickly. The policeman looked at the envelope, then tried to call him back, but he had gone. Since all messages which came for any of the policemen had to be put on the captain's desk first, he sent the envelope in to his office. The captain held it up to the light. When the policeman came back he called him in and made him open it in front of him. "Who is it from?" said the captain. The policeman scratched his head. He could not answer. "I see," said the captain. The next week he had the man transferred. Word came from the capital that he was to be sent to Rissani. "See how many friends you can make in the desert," the captain told him.

He would not listen to anything the policeman tried to say.

Salam went to Tangier. When he returned he heard that the policeman had been sent to the Sahara. This made him laugh a great deal. He went to the market and bought a half-grown goat. Then he invited Fatma Daifa and Abdallah and his wife and two of the brothers with their wives and children, and they killed the goat and ate it. It was nearly dawn by the time they all went home. Fatma Daifa did not want to go through the streets alone, and since Salam and Bou Ralem were too drunk to take her, she slept in the kitchen on the floor. When she woke up it was late, but Salam and Bou Ralem were still asleep. She got her things together, put on her *haik* and went out. As she came to the house of the woman with the little girl, she stood still and looked in. The woman saw her and was frightened. "What do you want?" she cried. Fatma Daifa knew she was meddling, but she thought this was the right thing to do for Salam. She pretended not to see the woman's frightened face, and she shook her fist back at the terrace, crying into the air: "Now I see what sort of man you are! You think you can cheat me? Listen to me! None of it's going to work, do you hear?" She walked on down the alley shouting: "None of it!" The other Jewish women came and stood around the door and sat on the curb in front of it. They agreed that if the old woman had fought with the two men there was no more danger from the magic, because only the old woman had the power to make it work. The mother of the little girl was happy, and the next day the child was playing in the mud with the others.

Salam went in and out of the alley as always, not noticing the children or the people. It was half a month before he said one day to Bou Ralem: "I think the Jews are feeling better. I saw the wrong Mimí out loose this morning." He was free again now that the policeman was gone, and he could carry his kif in his pocket without worrying when he went out through the streets to the café. The next time he saw Fatma Daifa she asked him about the Jews in his alley. "It's finished. They've forgotten," he said. "Good," she replied. Then she went to her house and got out the porcupine quill powder and the crow's wing and the seeds and all the rest of the packages. She put them into her basket, carried them to the market, and sold them there, and with the money she bought bread, oil, and eggs. She went home and cooked her dinner.

HE OF THE ASSEMBLY

HE OF THE ASSEMBLY

*He salutes all parts of the sky
and the earth where it is bright.
He thinks the color of the amethysts of Aguelmous will be dark
if it has rained in the valley of
Zerekten. The eye wants to sleep,
he says, but the head is no mattress. When it rained for three days
and water covered the flatlands
outside the ramparts, he slept by
the bamboo fence at the Café of
the Two Bridges.*

It seems there was a man named Ben Tajah who went to
Fez to visit his cousin. The day he came back he was walking
in the Djemaa el Fna, and he saw a letter lying on the
pavement. He picked it up and found that his name was
written on the envelope. He went to the Café of the Two
Bridges with the letter in his hand, sat down on a mat and
opened the envelope. Inside was a paper which read: 'The
sky trembles and the earth is afraid, and the two eyes are not
brothers.' Ben Tajah did not understand, and he was very
unhappy because his name was on the envelope. It made
him think that Satan was nearby. He of the Assembly was
sitting in the same part of the café. He was listening to

33

the wind in the telephone wires. The sky was almost empty of daytime light. "The eye wants to sleep," he thought, "but the head is no mattress. I know what that is, but I have forgotten it." Three days is a long time for rain to keep falling on flat bare ground. "If I got up and ran down the street," he thought, "a policeman would follow me and call to me to stop. I would run faster, and he would run after me. When he shot at me, I'd duck around the corners of houses." He felt the rough dried mud of the wall under his fingertips. "And I'd be running through the streets looking for a place to hide, but no door would be open, until finally I came to one door that was open, and I'd go in through the rooms and courtyards until finally I came to the kitchen. The old woman would be there." He stopped and wondered for a moment why an old woman should be there alone in the kitchen at that hour. She was stirring a big kettle of soup on the stove. "And I'd look for a place to hide there in the kitchen, and there'd be no place. And I'd be waiting to hear the policeman's footsteps, because he wouldn't miss the open door. And I'd look in the dark corner of the room where she kept the charcoal, but it wouldn't be dark enough. And the old woman would turn and look at me and say: 'If you're trying to get away, my boy, I can help you. Jump into the soup-kettle.'" The wind sighed in the telephone wires. Men came into the Café of the Two Bridges with their garments flapping. Ben Tajah sat on his mat. He had put the letter away, but first he had stared at it a long time. He of the Assembly leaned back and looked at the sky. "The old woman," he said to himself. "What is she trying to do? The soup is hot. It may be a trap. I may find there's no

34

way out, once I get down there." He wanted a pipe of kif, but
he was afraid the policeman would run into the kitchen
before he was able to smoke it. He said to the old woman:
"How can I get in? Tell me." And it seemed to him that he
heard footsteps in the street, or perhaps even in one of the
rooms of the house. He leaned over the stove and looked
down into the kettle. It was dark and very hot down in there.
Steam was coming up in clouds, and there was a thick smell
in the air that made it hard to breathe. "Quick!" said the old
woman, and she unrolled a rope ladder and hung it over the
edge of the kettle. He began to climb down, and she leaned
over and looked after him. "Until the other world!" he
shouted. And he climbed all the way down. There was a
rowboat below. When he was in it he tugged on the ladder
and the old woman began to pull it up. And at that instant
the policeman ran in, and two more were with him, and the
old woman had just the time to throw the ladder down into
the soup. "Now they are going to take her to the commissariat," he thought, "and the poor woman only did me a
favor." He rowed around in the dark for a few minutes, and
it was very hot. Soon he took off his clothes. For a while he
could see the round top of the kettle up above, like a port-
hole in the side of a ship, with the heads of the policemen
looking down in, but then it grew smaller as he rowed, until
it was only a light. Sometimes he could find it and sometimes he lost it, and finally it was gone. He was worried
about the old woman, and he thought he must find a way to
help her. No policeman can go into the Café of the Two
Bridges because it belongs to the Sultan's sister. This is why
there is so much kif smoke inside that a *berrada* can't fall

over even if it is pushed, and why most customers like to sit outside, and even there keep one hand on their money. As long as the thieves stay inside and their friends bring them food and kif, they are all right. One day police headquarters will forget to send a man to watch the café, or one man will leave five minutes before the other gets there to take his place. Outside everyone smokes kif too, but only for an hour or two—not all day and night like the ones inside. He of the Assembly had forgotten to light his *sebsi*. He was in a café where no policeman could come, and he wanted to go away to a kif world where the police were chasing him. "This is the way we are now," he thought. "We work backwards. If we have something good, we look for something bad instead." He lighted the *sebsi* and smoked it. Then he blew the hard ash out of the *chqaf*. It landed in the brook beside the second bridge. "The world is too good. We can only work forward if we make it bad again first." This made him sad, so he stopped thinking, and filled his *sebsi*. While he was smoking it, Ben Tajah looked in his direction, and although they were facing each other, He of the Assembly did not notice Ben Tajah until he got up and paid for his tea. Then he looked at him because he took such a long time getting up off the floor. He saw his face and thought: "That man has no one in the world." The idea made him feel cold. He filled his *sebsi* again and lighted it. He saw the man as he was going to go out of the café and walk alone down the long road outside the ramparts. In a little while he himself would have to go out to the *souks* to try and borrow money for dinner. When he smoked a lot of kif he did not like his aunt to see him, and he did not want to see her. "Soup and bread. No one can want more than that. Will thirty francs be enough the fourth time? The *qahouaji* wasn't satisfied last night. But he took it. And he went away and let me sleep. A Moslem, even in the city, can't refuse his brother shelter." He was not convinced, because he had been born in the mountains, and so he kept thinking back and forth in this way. He smoked many *chqofa,* and when he got up to go out into the street he found that the world had changed.

Ben Tajah was not a rich man. He lived alone in a room near Bab Doukkala, and he had a stall in the bazaars where he sold coathangers and chests. Often he did not open the shop because he was in bed with a liver attack. At such times he pounded on the floor from his bed, using a brass pestle, and the postman who lived downstairs brought him up some food. Sometimes he stayed in bed for a week at a time. Each morning and night the postman came in with a tray. The food was not very good because the postman's wife did not understand much about cooking. But he was glad to have it. Twice he had brought the postman a new chest to keep clothes and blankets in. One of the postman's wives a few years before had taken a chest with her when she had left him and gone back to her family in Kasba Tadla. Ben Tajah himself had tried having a wife for a while because he needed someone to get him regular meals and to wash his clothes, but the girl was from the mountains, and was wild. No matter how much he beat her she would not be tamed. Everything in the room got broken, and finally he had to put her out into the street. "No more women will get into my house," he told his friends in the bazaars, and they laughed. He took home many women, and one day he found that he had *en novar*. He knew that was a bad disease, because it stays in the blood and eats the nose from inside. "A man loses his nose only long after he has already lost his head." He asked a doctor for medicine. The doctor gave him a paper and told him to take it to the Pharmacie de l'Etoile. There he bought six vials of penicillin in a box. He took them home and tied each little bottle with a silk thread, stringing them so that they made a necklace. He wore this always around his neck, taking care that the glass vials touched his skin. He thought it likely that by now he was cured, but his cousin in Fez had just told him that he must go on wearing the medicine for another three months, or at least until the beginning of the moon of Chouwal. He had thought about this now and then on the way home, sitting in the bus for two days, and he had decided that his cousin was too cautious. He stood in the Djemaa el Fna a minute watching the trained monkeys, but the crowd pushed too much, so he walked on. When he got home he shut the door and put his hand in his pocket to pull out the envelope, because he wanted to look at it again inside his own room, and be sure that the name written on it was beyond a doubt his. But the letter was gone. He remembered the jostling in the Djemaa el Fna. Someone had reached into his pocket and imagined his hand was feeling money, and taken it. Yet Ben Tajah did not truly believe this. He was convinced that he would have known such a theft was happening. There had been a letter in his pocket. He was not even sure of that. He sat down on the cushions. "Two days in the bus," he thought. "Probably I'm tired. I found no letter." He searched in his pocket again, and it seemed to him he could still remember how the fold of the envelope had felt. "Why would it have my name on it? I never found any letter at all." Then he wondered if anyone had seen him in the café with the envelope in one hand and the sheet of paper in the other, looking at them both for such a long time. He stood up. He wanted to go back to the Café of the Two Bridges and ask the *qahouaji:* "Did you see me an hour ago? Was I looking at a letter?" If the *qahouaji* said: "Yes," then the letter was real. He repeated the words aloud: "The sky trembles, and the earth is afraid, and the two eyes are not brothers." In the silence afterwards the memory of the sound of the words frightened him. "If there was no letter, where are these words from?" And he shivered because the answer to that was: "From Satan." He was about to open the door when a new fear stopped him. The *qahouaji* might say: "No," and this would be still worse, because it would mean that the words had been put directly into his head by Satan, that Satan had chosen him to reveal Himself to. In that case, He might appear at any moment. *"Ach haddou laillaha ill' Allah ... "* he prayed, holding his two forefingers up, one on each side of him. He sat down again and did not move. In the street the children were crying. He did not want to hear the *qahouaji* say: "No. You had no letter." If he knew that Satan was coming to tempt him, he would have that much less power to keep Him away with his prayers, because he would be more afraid.

He of the Assembly stood. Behind him was a wall. In his hand was the *sebsi.* Over his head was the sky, which he felt was about to burst into light. He was leaning back looking at it. It was dark on the earth, but there was still

light up there behind the stars. Ahead of him was the pissoir
of the Carpenters' Souk which the French had put there.
People said only Jews used it. It was made of tin, and there
was a puddle in front of it that reflected the sky and the top
of the pissoir. It looked like a boat in the water. Or like a pier
where boats land. Without moving from where he stood, He
of the Assembly saw it approaching slowly. He was going
toward it. And he remembered he was naked, and put his
hand over his sex. In a minute the rowboat would be bump-
ing against the pier. He steadied himself on his legs and
waited. But at that moment a large cat ran out of the shadow
of the wall and stopped in the middle of the street to turn
and look at him with an evil face. He was not sure what had
happened, and he stood very still looking at the ground. He
looked back at the pissoir reflected in the puddle and
thought: "It was a cat on the shore, nothing else." But the
cat's eyes had frightened him. Instead of being like cats-eyes,
they had looked like the eyes of a person who was interested
in him. He made himself forget he had had this thought. He
was still waiting for the rowboat to touch the landing pier,
but nothing had happened. It was going to stay where it
was, near the shore but not near enough to touch. He stood
still a long time, waiting for something to happen. Then he
began to walk very fast down the street toward the bazaars.
He had just remembered that the old woman was in the
police station. He wanted to help her, but first he had to find
out where they had taken her. "I'll have to go to every police
station in the Medina," he thought, and he was not hungry
any more. It was one thing to promise himself he would
help her when he was far from land, and another when he

was a few doors from a commissariat. He walked by the entrance. Two policemen stood in the doorway. He kept walking. The street curved and he was alone. "This night is going to be a jewel in my crown," he said, and he turned quickly to the left and went along a dark passageway. At the end he saw flames, and he knew that Mustapha would be there tending the fire of the bakery. He crawled into the mud hut where the oven was. "Ah, the jackal has come back from the forest!" said Mustapha. He of the Assembly shook his head. "This is a bad world," he told Mustapha. "I've got no money," Mustapha said. He of the Assembly did not understand. "Everything goes backwards," he said. "It's bad now, and we have to make it still worse if we want to go forwards." Mustapha saw that He of the Assembly was *mkiyif ma rassou* and was not interested in money. He looked at him in a more friendly way and said: "Secrets are not between friends. Talk." He of the Assembly told him that an old woman had done him a great favor, and because of that three policemen had arrested her and taken her to the police station. "You must go for me to the commissariat and ask them if they have an old woman there." He pulled out his *sebsi* and took a very long time filling it. When he finished it he smoked it himself and did not offer any to Mustapha, because Mustapha never offered him any of his. "You see how full of kif my head is," he said laughing. "I can't go." Mustapha laughed too and said it would not be a good idea, and that he would go for him.

"I was there, and I heard him go away for a long time, so long that he had to be gone, and yet he was still there, and his footsteps were still going away. He went away and there was nobody. There was the fire and I moved away from it. I wanted to hear a sound like a muezzin crying *Allah akbar!* or a French plane from the Pilot Base flying over the Medina, or news on the radio. It wasn't there. And when the wind came in the door it was made of dust high as a man. A night to be chased by dogs in the Mellah. I looked in the fire and I saw an eye in there, like the eye that's left when you burn *chibb* and you knew there was a *djinn* in the house. I got up and stood. The fire was making a noise like a voice. I think it was talking. I went out and walked along the street. I walked a long time and I came to Bab el Khemiss. It was dark there and the wind was cold. I went to the wall where the camels were lying and stood there. Sometimes the men have fires and play songs on their *aouadas*. But they were asleep. All snoring. I walked again and went to the gate and looked out. The big trucks went by full of vegetables and I thought I would like to be on a truck and ride all night. Then in another city I would be a soldier and go to Algeria. Everything would be good if we had a war. I thought a long time. Then I was so cold I turned around and walked again. It was as cold as the belly of the oldest goat of Ijoukak. I thought I heard a muezzin and I stopped and listened. The only thing I heard was the water running in the *seguia* that carries the water out to the gardens. It was near the *mçid* of Moulay Boujemaa. I heard the water running by and I felt cold. Then I knew I was cold because I was afraid. In my head I was thinking: if something should happen that never happened before, what would I do? You want to laugh? Hashish in your heart and wind in your head. You think it's like your grandmother's prayer-mat. This is the truth. This isn't a dream brought back from another world past the customs like a teapot from Mecca. I heard the water and I was afraid. There were some trees by the path ahead of me. You know at night sometimes it's good to pull out the *sebsi* and smoke. I smoked and I started to walk. And then I heard something. Not a muezzin. Something that sounded like my name. But it came up from below, from the *seguia, Allah istir!* And I walked with my head down. I heard it again saying my name, a voice like water, like the wind moving the leaves in the trees, a woman. It was a woman calling me. The wind was in the trees and the water was running, but there was a woman too. You think it's kif. No, she was calling my name. Now and then, not very loud. When I was under the trees it was louder, and I heard that the voice was my mother's. I heard that the way I can hear you. Then I knew the cat was not a cat, and I knew that Aïcha Qandicha wanted me. I thought of other nights when perhaps she had been watching me from the eyes of a cat or a donkey. I knew she was not going to catch me. Nothing in the seven skies could make me turn around. But I was cold and afraid and when I licked my lips my tongue had no spit on it. I was under the *safsaf* trees and I thought: she's going to reach down and try to touch me. But she can't touch me from the front and I won't turn around, not even if I hear a pistol. I remembered how the policeman had fired at me and how I'd found only one door open. I began to yell: 'You threw me the ladder and told me to climb down! You brought me here! The filthiest whore in the Mellah, with the pus coming out of her, is a thousand times cleaner than you, daughter of all the padronas and dogs in seven worlds!' I got past

43

the trees and I began to run. I called up to the sky so she could hear my voice behind: 'I hope the police put a hose in your mouth and pump you full of salt water until you crack open!' I thought: tomorrow I'm going to buy *fasoukh* and *tib* and *nidd* and *hasalouba* and *mska* and all the *bakhour* in the Djemaa, and put them in the *mijmah* and burn them, and walk back and forth over the *mijmah* ten times slowly, so the smoke can clean out all my clothes. Then I'll see if there's an eye in the ashes afterwards. If there is, I'll do it all over again right away. And every Thursday I'll buy the *bakhour* and every Friday I'll burn it. That will be strong enough to keep her away. If I could find a window and look through and see what they're doing to the old woman! If only they could kill her! I kept running. There were a few people in the streets. I didn't look to see where I was going, but I went to the street near Mustapha's oven where the commissariat was. I stopped running before I got to the door. The one standing there saw me before that. He stepped out and raised his arm. He said to me: 'Come here.'"

He of the Assembly ran. He felt as though he were on horseback. He did not feel his legs moving. He saw the road coming toward him and the doors going by. The policeman had not shot at him yet, but it was worse than the other time because he was very close behind and he was blowing his whistle. "The policeman is old. At least thirty-five. I can run faster." But from any street others could come. It was dangerous and he did not want to think about danger. He of the Assembly let songs come into his head. When it rains in the valley of Zerekten the amethysts are darker in Aguelmous. The eye wants sleep but the head is no mattress. It was a

44

song. Ah, my brother, the ink on the paper is like smoke in the air. What words are there to tell how long a night can be? Drunk with love, I wander in the dark. He was running through the dye-souk, and he splashed into a puddle. The whistle blew again behind him, like a crazy bird screaming. The sound made him feel like laughing, but that did not mean he was not afraid. He thought: "If I'm seventeen I can run faster. That has to be true." It was very dark ahead. He had to slow his running. There was no time for his eyes to get used to the dark. He nearly ran into the wall of the shop at the end of the street. He turned to the right and saw the narrow alley ahead of him. The police had tied the old woman naked to a table with her thin legs wide apart and were sliding electrodes up inside her. He ran ahead. He could see the course of the alley now even in the dark. Then he stopped dead, moved to the wall, and stood still. He heard the footsteps slowing down. "He's going to turn to the left." And he whispered aloud: "It ends that way." The footsteps stopped and there was silence. The policeman was looking into the silence and listening into the dark to the left and to the right. He of the Assembly could not see him or hear him, but he knew that was what he was doing. He did not move. When it rains in the valley of Zerekten. A hand seized his shoulder. He opened his mouth and swiftly turned, but the man had moved and was pushing him from the side. He felt the wool of the man's *djellaba* against the back of his hand. He had gone through a door and the man had shut it without making any noise. Now they both stood still in the dark, listening to the policeman walking quickly by outside the door. Then the man struck a match. He was

facing the other way, and there was a flight of stairs ahead.
The man did not turn around, but he said, "Come up," and
they both climbed the stairs. At the top the man took out a
key and opened a door. He of the Assembly stood in the
doorway while the man lit a candle. He liked the room
because it had many mattresses and cushions and a white
sheepskin under the tea-tray in the corner of the floor. The
man turned around and said: "Sit down." His face looked
serious and kind and unhappy. He of the Assembly had
never seen it before, but he knew it was not the face of a
policeman. He of the Assembly pulled out his *sebsi*.

Ben Tajah looked at the boy and asked him: "What did
you mean when you said down there: 'It ends that way?' I
heard you say it." The boy was embarrassed. He smiled and
looked at the floor. Ben Tajah felt happy to have him there.
He had been standing outside the door downstairs in the
dark for a long time, trying to make himself go to the Café of
the Two Bridges and talk to the *qahouaji*. In his mind it was
almost as though he had already been there and spoken with
him. He had heard the *qahouaji* telling him that he had
seen no letter, and he had felt his own dismay. He had not
wanted to believe that, but he would be willing to say yes, I
made a mistake and there was no letter, if only he could find
out where the words had come from. For the words were
certainly in his head: " ... and the two eyes are not brothers." That was like a footprint found in the garden the
morning after a bad dream, the proof that there had been a
reason for the dream, that something had been there after
all. Ben Tajah had not been able to go or to stay. He had
started and stopped so many times that now, although he

46

did not know it, he was very tired. When a man is tired he mistakes the hopes of children for the knowledge of men. It seemed to him that He of the Assembly's words had a meaning all for him. Even though the boy might not know it, he could have been sent by Allah to help him at that minute. In a nearby street a police whistle blew. The boy looked at him. Ben Tajah did not care very much what the answer would be, but he said: "Why are they looking for you?" The boy held out his lighted *sebsi* and his *mottoui* fat with kif. He did not want to talk because he was listening. Ben Tajah smoked kif only when a friend offered it to him, but he understood that the police had begun once more to try to enforce their law against kif. Each year they arrested people for a few weeks, and then stopped arresting them. He looked at the boy, and decided that probably he smoked too much. With the *sebsi* in his hand he was sitting very still listening to the voices of some passers-by in the street below. "I know who he is," one said. "I've got his name from Mustapha." "The baker?" "That's the one." They walked on. The boy's expression was so intense that Ben Tajah said to him: "It's nobody. Just people." He was feeling happy because he was certain that Satan would not appear before him as long as the boy was with him. He said quietly: "Still you haven't told me why you said: 'It ends that way.'" The boy filled his *sebsi* slowly and smoked all the kif in it. "I meant," he said, "thanks to Allah. Praise the sky and the earth where it is bright. What else can you mean when something ends?" Ben Tajah nodded his head. Pious thoughts can be of as much use for keeping Satan at a distance as camphor or *bakhour* dropped onto hot coals.

47

Each holy word is worth a high column of smoke, and the eyelids do not smart afterward. "He has a good heart," thought Ben Tajah, "even though he is probably a guide for the Nazarenes." And he asked himself why it would not be possible for the boy to have been sent to protect him from Satan. "Probably not. But it could be." The boy offered him the *sebsi*. He took it and smoked it. After that Ben Tajah began to think that he would like to go to the Café of the Two Bridges and speak to the *qahouaji* about the letter. He felt that if the boy went with him the *qahouaji* might say there had been a letter, and that even if the man could not remember, he would not mind so much because he would be less afraid. He waited until he thought the boy was not nervous about going into the street, and then he said: "Let's go out and get some tea." "Good," said the boy. He was not afraid of the police if he was with Ben Tajah. They went through the empty streets, crossed the Djemaa el Fna and the garden beyond. When they were near the café, Ben Tajah said to the boy: "Do you know the Café of the Two Bridges?" The boy said he always sat there, and Ben Tajah was not surprised. It seemed to him that perhaps he had even seen him there. He seized the boy's arm. "Were you there today?" he asked him. The boy said, "Yes," and turned to look at him. He let go of the arm. "Nothing," he said. "Did you ever see me there?" They came to the gate of the café and Ben Tajah stopped walking. "No," the boy said. They went across the first bridge and then the second bridge, and sat down in a corner. Not many people were left outside. Those inside were making a great noise. The *qahouaji* brought the tea and went away again. Ben Tajah did not say anything to him about the letter. He wanted to drink the tea quietly and leave trouble until later.

When the muezzin called from the minaret of the Koutoubia, He of the Assembly thought of being in the Agdal. The great mountains were ahead of him and the olive trees stood in rows on each side of him. Then he heard the trickle of water and he remembered the *seguia* that is there in the Agdal, and he swiftly came back to the Café of the Two Bridges. Aïcha Qandicha can only be where there are trees by running water. "She comes only for single men by trees and fresh moving water. Her arms are gold and she calls in the voice of the most cherished one." Ben Tajah gave him the *sebsi*. He filled it and smoked it. "When a man sees her face he will never see another woman's face. He will make love with her all the night, and every night, and in the sunlight by the walls, before the eyes of children. Soon he will be an empty pod and he will leave this world for his home in Jehennem." The last carriage went by, taking the last tourists down the road beside the ramparts to their rooms in the Mamounia. He of the Assembly thought: "The eye wants to sleep. But this man is alone in the world. He wants to talk all night. He wants to tell me about his wife and how he beat her and how she broke everything. Why do I want to know all these things? He is a good man but he has no head." Ben Tajah was sad. He said: "What have I done? Why does Satan choose me?" Then at last he told the boy about the letter, about how he wondered if it had had his name on the envelope and how he was not even sure there had been a letter. When he finished he looked sadly at the boy. "And you didn't see me." He of the Assembly shut his eyes and kept them shut for a while. When he opened them again he said: "Are you alone in the world?" Ben Tajah stared at him and did not speak. The boy laughed. "I did see you," he said, "but you had no letter. I saw you when you were getting up and I thought you were old. Then I saw you were not old. That's all I saw." "No, it isn't," Ben Tajah said. "You saw that I was alone." He of the Assembly shrugged. "Who knows?" He filled the *sebsi* and handed it to Ben Tajah. The kif was in Ben Tajah's head. His eyes were small. He of the Assembly listened to the wind in the telephone wires, took back the *sebsi* and filled it again. Then he said: "You think Satan is coming to make trouble for you because you're alone in the world. I see that. Get a wife or somebody to be with you always, and you won't think about it any more. That's true. Because Satan doesn't come to men like you." He of the Assembly did not believe this himself. He knew that Father Satan can come for anyone in the world, but he hoped to live with Ben Tajah, so he would not have to borrow money in the *souks* to buy food. Ben Tajah drank some tea. He did not want the boy to see that his face was happy. He felt that the boy was right, and that there never had been a letter. "Two days on a bus is a long time. A man can get very tired," he said. Then he called the *qahouaji* and told him to bring two more glasses of tea. He of the Assembly gave him the *sebsi*. He knew that Ben Tajah wanted to stay as long as possible in the Café of the Two Bridges. He put his finger into the *mottoui*. The kif was almost gone. "We can talk," he said. "Not much kif is in the *mottoui*." The *qahouaji* brought the tea. They talked for an hour or more. The *qahouaji* slept and snored. They talked about Satan and the bad thing it is to live alone, to wake up in the dark and know there is no one else nearby. Many times He of the Assembly told Ben Tajah that he must not worry. The kif was all gone. He held his empty *mottoui* in his hand. He did not understand how he had got back to the town without climbing up out of the soup kettle. Once he said to Ben Tajah: "I never climbed back up." Ben Tajah looked at him and said he did not understand. He of the Assembly told him the story. Ben Tajah laughed. He said: "You smoke too much kif, brother." He of the Assembly put his *sebsi* into his pocket. "And you don't smoke and you're afraid of Satan," he told Ben Tajah. "No!" Ben Tajah shouted. "By Allah! No more! But one thing is in my head, and I can't put it out. The sky trembles and the earth is afraid, and the two eyes are not brothers. Did you ever hear those words? Where did they come from?" Ben Tajah looked hard at the boy. He of the Assembly understood that these had been the words on the paper, and he felt cold in the middle of his back because he had never heard them before and they sounded evil. He knew, too, that he must not let Ben Tajah know this. He began to laugh. Ben Tajah took hold of his knee and shook it. His face was troubled. "Did you ever hear them?" He of the Asembly went on laughing. Ben Tajah shook his leg so hard that he stopped and said: "Yes!" When Ben Tajah waited and he said nothing more, he saw the man's face growing angry, and so he said: "Yes, I've heard them. But will you tell me what happened to me and how I got out of the soup-kettle if I tell you about those words?" Ben Tajah understood that the kif was going away from the boy's head. But he saw that it had not all gone, or he would not have been asking that question. And he said: "Wait a while for the answer to that question." He of the Assembly woke the *qahouaji* and Ben Tajah paid him, and they went out of the café. They did not talk while they walked. When they got to the Mouassine mosque, Ben Tajah held out his hand to say goodnight, but He of the Assembly said: "I'm looking in my head for the place I heard your words. I'll walk to your door with you. Maybe I'll remember." Ben Tajah said: "May Allah help you find it." And he took his arm and they walked to Ben Tajah's door while He of the Assembly said nothing. They stood outside the door in the dark. "Have you found it?" said Ben Tajah. "Almost," said He of the Assembly. Ben Tajah thought that perhaps when the kif had gone out of the boy's head he might be able to tell him about the words. He wanted to know how the boy's head was, and so he said: "Do you still want to know how you got out of the soup-kettle?" He of the Assembly laughed. "You said you would tell me later," he told Ben Tajah. "I will," said Ben Tajah. "Come upstairs. Since we have to wait we can sit down." Ben Tajah opened the door and they went upstairs. This time He of the Assembly sat down on Ben Tajah's bed. He yawned and stretched. It was a good bed. He was glad it was not the mat by the bamboo fence at the Café of the Two Bridges. "And so, tell me how I got out of the soup-kettle," he said laughing. Ben Tajah said: "You're still asking me that? Have you thought of the words?" "I know the words," the boy said. "The sky trembles ... " Ben Tajah did not want him to say them again. "Where did you hear them? What are they? That's what I want to know." The boy shook his head.

Then he sat up very straight and looked beyond Ben Tajah, beyond the wall of the room, beyond the streets of the Medina, beyond the gardens, toward the mountains where the people speak Tachelhait. He remembered being a little boy. "This night is a jewel in my crown," he thought. "It went this way." And he began to sing, making up a melody for the words Ben Tajah had told him. When he had finished "... and the two eyes are not brothers," he added a few more words of his own and stopped singing. "That's all I remember of the song," he said. Ben Tajah clapped his hands together hard. "A song!" he cried. "I must have heard it on the radio." He of the Assembly shrugged. "They play it sometimes," he said. "I've made him happy," he thought. "But I won't ever tell him another lie. That's the only one. What I'm going to do now is not the same as lying." He got up off the bed and went to the window. The muezzins were calling the *fjer*. "It's almost morning," he said to Ben Tajah. "I still have kif in my head." "Sit down," said Ben Tajah. He was sure now there had been no letter. He of the Assembly took off his *djellaba* and got into bed. Ben Tajah looked at him in surprise. Then he undressed and got into bed beside him. He left the candle burning on the floor beside the bed. He meant to stay awake, but he went to sleep because he was not used to smoking kif and the kif was in his head. He of the Assembly did not believe he was asleep. He lay for a long time without moving. He listened to the voices of the muezzins, and he thought that the man beside him would speak or move. When he saw that Ben Tajah was surely asleep, he was angry. "This is how he treats a friend who has made him happy. He forgets his trouble and his

53

friend too." He thought about it more and he was angrier. The muezzins were still calling the *fjer*. "Before they stop, or he will hear." Very slowly he got out of the bed. He put on his *djellaba* and opened the door. Then he went back and took all the money out of Ben Tajah's pockets. In with the banknotes was an envelope that was folded. It had Ben Tajah's name written across it. He pulled out the piece of paper inside and held it near the candle, and then he looked at it as he would have looked at a snake. The words were written there. Ben Tajah's face was turned toward the wall and he was snoring. He of the Assembly held the paper above the flame and burned it, and then he burned the envelope. He blew the black paper-ashes across the floor. Without making any noise he ran downstairs and let himself out into the street. He shut the door. The money was in his pocket and he walked fast to his aunt's house. His aunt awoke and was angry for a while. Finally he said: "It was raining. How could I come home? Let me sleep." He had a little kif hidden under his pillow. He smoked a pipe. Then he looked across his sleep to the morning and thought: "A pipe of kif before breakfast gives a man the strength of a hundred camels in the courtyard."

THE STORY OF LAHCEN AND IDIR

THE STORY OF LAHCEN AND IDIR

Two friends, Lahcen and Idir, were walking on the
beach at Merkala. By the rocks stood a girl, and her *djellaba*
blew in the wind. Lahcen and Idir stopped walking when
they saw her. They stood still, looking at her. Lahcen said:
"Do you know that one?" "No. I never saw her." "Let's go
over," said Lahcen. They looked up and down the beach for
a man who might be with the girl, but there was no one. "A
whore," said Lahcen. When they got closer to the girl, they
saw that she was very young. Lahcen laughed. "This is
easy." "How much have you got?" Idir asked him. "You
think I'm going to pay her?" cried Lahcen.

Idir understood that Lahcen meant to beat her. ("If you
don't pay a whore you have to beat her.") And he did not like
the idea, because they had done it before together, and it
nearly always meant trouble later. Her sister or someone in
her family went to the police and complained, and in the
end everybody was in jail. Being shut into prison made Idir
nervous. He tried to keep out of it, and he was usually able
to. The difference between Lahcen and Idir was that Lahcen
liked to drink and Idir smoked kif. Kif smokers want to stay
quiet in their heads, and drinkers are not like that. They
want to break things.

57

A Hundred Camels in the Courtyard

Lahcen rubbed his groin and spat onto the sand. Idir knew he was going over the moves in the game he was going to play with the girl, planning when and where he would knock her down. He was worried. The girl looked the other way. She held down the skirt of her *djellaba* so the wind would not blow it. Lahcen said: "Wait here." He went on to her and Idir saw her lips moving as she spoke to him, for she wore no veil. All her teeth were gold. Idir hated women with gold teeth because at fourteen he had been in love with a gold-toothed whore named Zohra, who never had paid him any attention. He said to himself: "He can have her." Besides, he did not want to be with them when the trouble began. He stood still until Lahcen whistled to him. Then he went over to where they stood. "Ready?" Lahcen asked. He took the girl's arm and started to walk along beside the rocks. "It's late. I've got to go," Idir told him. Lahcen looked surprised, but he said nothing. "Some other day," Idir told Lahcen, looking at him and trying to warn him. The girl laughed spitefully, as if she thought that might shame him into coming along.

He was glad he had decided to go home. When he went by the Mendoub's fig orchard a dog barked at him. He threw a rock at it and hit it.

The next morning Lahcen came to Idir's room. His eyes were red from the wine he had been drinking. He sat down on the floor and pulled out a handkerchief that had a knot tied in one corner. He untied the knot and let a gold ring fall out into his lap. Picking up the ring, he handed it to Idir. "For you. I got it cheap." Idir saw that Lahcen wanted him to take the ring, and he put it on his finger, saying: "May Allah give you health." Lahcen rubbed his hand across his chin and yawned. Then he said: "I saw you look at me, and afterward when we got to the quarry I thought that would be the best place. And then I remembered the night the police took us at Bou Khach Khach, and I remembered you looking at me. I turned around and left her there. Garbage!"

"So you're not in jail and you're drunk," said Idir, and he laughed.

"That's true," said Lahcen. "And that's why I give you the ring."

Idir knew the ring was worth at least fifty dirhams, and he could sell it if he needed money badly. That would end his friendship with Lahcen, but there would be no help for it.

Sometimes Lahcen came by in the evening with a bottle of wine. He would drink the whole bottle while Idir smoked his kif pipe, and they would listen to the radio until the end of the program at twelve o'clock. Afterward, very late, they would walk through the streets of Dradeb to a garage where a friend of Lahcen was a night watchman. When the moon was full, it was brighter than the street lights. With no moon, there was nobody in the streets, and in a few late cafés the men told one another about what thieves had done, and how there were more of them than ever before. This was because there was almost no work to be had anywhere, and the country people were selling their cows and sheep to be able to pay their taxes, and then coming to the city. Lahcen and Idir worked now and then, whenever they found something to do. They had a little money, they always ate, and

A Hundred Camels in the Courtyard

Lahcen sometimes was able to afford his bottle of Spanish
wine. Idir's kif was more of a problem, because each time the
police decided to enforce the law they had made against it, it
grew very scarce and the price went up. Then when there
was plenty to be had, because the police were busy looking
for guns and rebels instead, the price stayed high. He did not
smoke any less, but he smoked by himself in his room. If you
smoke in a café, there is always someone who has left his kif
at home and wants to use yours. He told his friends at the
Café Nadjah that he had given up kif, and he never accepted
a pipe when it was offered to him.

Back in his room in the early evening, with the window
open and the sleepy sounds of the town coming up, for it
was summer and the voices of people filled the streets, Idir
sat in the chair he had bought and put his feet on the
windowsill. That way he could see the sky as he smoked.
Lahcen would come in and talk. Now and then they went
together to Emsallah to a *barraca* there near the slaughter
house where two sisters lived with their feeble-minded
mother. They would get the mother drunk and put her to
bed in the inner room. Then they would get the girls drunk
and spend the night with them, without paying. The cognac was expensive, but it did not cost as much as whores
would have.

In midsummer, at the time of Sidi Kacem, it suddenly
grew very hot. People set up tents made of sheets on the roofs
of their houses and cooked and slept there. At night in the
moonlight Idir could see all the roofs, each one with its box
of sheets flapping in the wind, and inside the sheets the red
light made by the fire in the pot. Daytimes, the sun shining

on the sea of white sheets hurt his eyes, and he remembered
not to look out when he passed the window as he moved
about his room. He would have liked to live in a more
expensive room, one with a blind to keep out the light.
There was no way of being protected from the bright
summer day that filled the sky outside, and he waited with
longing for dusk. His custom was not to smoke kif before
the sun went down. He did not like it in the daytime, above
all in summer when the air is hot and the light is powerful.
When each day came up hotter than the one before it, he
decided to buy enough food and kif to last several days, and
to shut himself into his room until it got cooler. He had
worked two days at the port that week and had some money.
He put the food on the table and locked the door. Then he
took the key out of the lock and threw it into the drawer of
the table. Lying with the packages and cans in his market
basket was a large bundle of kif wrapped in a newspaper. He
unfolded it, took out a sheaf and sniffed of it. For the next
two hours he sat on the floor picking off the leaves and
cutting them on a breadboard, sifting, and cutting, again
and again. Once, as the sun reached him, he had to move to
get out of its heat. By the time the sun went down he had
enough ready for three or four days. He got up off the floor
and sat in his chair with his pouch and his pipe in his lap,
and smoked, while the radio played the Chleuh music that
was always broadcast at this hour for the Soussi shopkeep-
ers. In cafés men often got up and turned it off. Idir enjoyed
it. Kif smokers usually like it, because of the *naqous* that
always pounds the same design.

A Hundred Camels in the Courtyard

The music played a long time, and Idir thought of the market at Tiznit and the mosque with the tree trunks sticking out of its mud walls. He looked down at the floor. The room still had daylight in it. He opened his eyes wide. A small bird was walking slowly along the floor. He jumped up. The kif pipe fell, but its bowl did not break. Before the bird had time to move, he had put his hand over it. Even when he held it between his two hands it did not struggle. He looked at it, and thought it was the smallest bird he had ever seen. Its head was gray, and its wings were black and white. It looked at him, and it did not seem afraid. He sat down in the chair with the bird in his lap. When he lifted his hand it stayed still. "It's a young bird and can't fly," he thought. He smoked several pipes of kif. The bird did not move. The sun had gone down and the houses were growing blue in the evening light. He stroked the bird's head with his thumb. Then he took the ring from his little finger and slipped it over the smooth feathers of its head. The bird paid no attention. "A gold collar for the sultan of birds," he said. He smoked some more kif and looked at the sky. Then he began to be hungry, and he thought the bird might like some breadcrumbs. He put his pipe down on the table and tried to take the ring from the bird's head. It would not come off over the feathers. He pulled at it, and the bird fluttered its wings and struggled. For a second he let go of it, and in that instant it flew straight from his lap into the sky. Idir jumped up and stood watching it. When it was gone, he began to smile. "The son of a whore!" he whispered.

He prepared his food and ate it. After that he sat in the chair smoking and thinking about the bird. When Lahcen came he told him the story. "He was waiting all the time for a chance to steal something," he said. Lahcen was a little drunk and he was angry. "So he stole my ring!" he cried. "Ah," said Idir. "Yours? I thought you gave it to me."

"I'm not crazy yet," Lahcen told him. He went away still angry, and did not return for more than a week. The morning he came into the room Idir was certain that he was going to begin to talk again about the ring, and he quickly handed him a pair of shoes he had bought from a friend the day before. "Do these fit you?" he asked him. Lahcen sat down in the chair, put them on, and found they did fit. "They need new bottoms, but the tops are like new," Idir told him. "The tops are good," said Lahcen. He felt of the leather and squeezed it between his thumb and fingers. "Take them," said Idir. Lahcen was pleased, and he said nothing about the ring that day. When he got the shoes to his room he looked carefully at them and decided to spend the money that it would cost to have new soles made.

The next day he went to a Spanish cobbler, who agreed to repair the shoes for fifteen dirhams. "Ten," said Lahcen. After a long discussion the cobbler lowered his price to thirteen, and he left the shoes there, saying that he would call for them in a week. The same afternoon he was walking through Sidi Bouknadel, and he saw a girl. They talked together for two hours or more, standing not very near to each other beside the wall, and looking down at the ground so that no one could see they were talking. The girl was from Meknes, and that was why he had never seen her before. She was visiting her aunt, who lived there in the quarter, and soon her sister was coming from Meknes. She looked to him the best thing he had seen that year, but of course he could not be sure of her nose and mouth because her veil hid them. He got her to agree to meet him at the same place the next day. This time they took a walk along the Hafa, and he could see that she would be willing. But she would not tell him where her aunt's house was.

Only two days later he got her to his room. As he had expected, she was beautiful. That night he was very happy, but in the morning when she had gone, he understood that he wanted to be with her all the time. He wanted to know what her aunt's house was like and how she was going to pass her day. In this way a bad time began for Lahcen. He was happy only when she was with him and he could get into bed and see her lying on one side of him and a bottle of cognac on the other, upright on the floor beside his pillow, where he could reach it easily. Each day when she had gone he lay thinking about all the men she might be going to see before she came back to him. When he talked about it to her she laughed and said she spent all her time with her aunt and sister, who now had arrived from Meknes. But he could not stop worrying about it.

Two weeks went by before he remembered to go and get his shoes. On his way to the cobbler's he thought about how he would solve his problem. He had an idea that Idir could help him. If he brought Idir and the girl together and left them alone, Idir would tell him afterward everything that had happened. If she let Idir take her to bed, then she was a whore and could be treated like a whore. He would give her a good beating and then make it up with her, because she was too good to throw away. But he had to know whether she was really his, or whether she would go with others.

When the cobbler handed him his shoes, he saw that they looked almost like new, and he was pleased. He paid the thirteen dirhams and took the shoes home. That night when he was going to put them on to wear to the café, he found that his feet would not go into them. They were much too small. The cobbler had cut down the last in order to stitch on the new soles. He put his old shoes back on, went out, and slammed the door. That night he had a quarrel with the girl. It took him until almost dawn to stop her crying. When the sun came up and she was asleep, he lay with his arms folded behind his head looking at the ceiling, thinking that the shoes had cost him thirteen dirhams and now he was going to have to spend the day trying to sell them. He got rid of the girl early and went in to Bou Araqia with the shoes. No one would give him more than eight dirhams for them. In the afternoon he went to the Joteya and sat in the shade of a grapevine, waiting for the buyers and sellers to arrive. A man from the mountains finally offered him ten dirhams, and he sold the shoes. "Three dirhams gone for nothing," he thought when he put the money into his pocket. He was angry, but instead of blaming the cobbler, he felt that the fault was Idir's.

That afternoon he saw Idir, and he told him he would bring a friend with him to Idir's room after the evening meal. Then he went home and drank cognac. When the girl arrived he had finished the bottle, and he was drunk and more unhappy than ever. "Don't take it off," he told her when she began to unfasten her veil. "We're going out." She said nothing. They took the back streets to Idir's room.

A Hundred Camels in the Courtyard

Idir sat in his chair listening to the radio. He had not expected a girl, and when he saw her take off her veil the beating of his heart made his head ache. He told her to sit in the chair, and then he paid no more attention to her and sat on the bed talking only with Lahcen, who did not look at her either. Soon Lahcen got up. "I'm going out to get some cigarettes," he said. "I'll be right back." He shut the door after him, and Idir quickly went and locked it. He smiled at the girl and sat on the table beside her, looking down at her. Now and then he smoked a pipe of kif. He wondered why Lahcen was taking so long. Finally he said: "He's not coming back, you know." The girl laughed and shrugged. He jumped up, took her hand, and led her to the bed.

In the morning when they were getting dressed, she told him she lived at the Hotel Sevilla. It was a small Moslem hotel in the center of the Medina. He took her there and left her. "Will you come tonight?" she asked him. Idir frowned. He was thinking of Lahcen. "Don't wait for me after midnight," he said. On his way home he stopped at the Café Nadjah. Lahcen was there. His eyes were red and he looked as though he had not slept at all. Idir had the feeling that he had been waiting for him to appear, for when he came into the café Lahcen quickly got up and paid the *qahouaji*. They walked down the main street of Dradeb without saying anything, and when they got to the road that leads to the Merkala beach, they turned down it, still without speaking.

It was low tide. They walked on the wet sand while the small waves broke at their feet. Lahcen smoked a cigarette and threw stones into the water. Finally he spoke. "How was it?"

66

The Story of Lahcen and Idir

Idir shrugged, tried to keep his voice flat. "All right for one night," he said. Lahcen was ready to say carelessly: "Or even two." But then he realized that Idir did not want to talk about the night, which meant that it had been a great event for him. And when he looked at his face he was certain that Idir wanted the girl for himself. He was sure he had already lost her to him, but he did not know why he had not thought of that in the beginning. Now he forgot the true reason why he had wanted to take her to Idir.

"You thought I brought her just to be good to you!" he cried. "No sidi! I left her there to see if you were a friend. And I see what kind of friend you are! A scorpion!" He seized the front of Idir's garments and struck him in the face. Idir moved backward a few steps, and got ready to fight. He understood that Lahcen had seen the truth, and that now there was nothing at all to say, and nothing to do but fight. When they were both bloody and panting, he looked for a flash at Lahcen's face, and saw that he was dizzy and could not see very well. He drew back, put his head down, and with all his force ran into Lahcen, who lost his balance and fell onto the sand. Then quickly he kicked him in the head with the heel of his shoe. He left him lying there and went home.

In a little while Lahcen began to hear the waves breaking on the sand near him. "I must kill him," he thought. "He sold my ring. Now I must go and kill him." Instead, he took off his clothes and bathed in the sea, and when he had finished, he lay in the sun on the sand all day and slept. In the evening he went and got very drunk.

At eleven o'clock Idir went to the Hotel Sevilla. The girl was sitting in a wicker chair by the front door, waiting for him. She looked carefully at the cuts on his face. Under her veil he saw her smile.

"You fought?" Idir nodded his head. "How is he?" He shrugged. This made her laugh. "He was always drunk, anyway," she said. Idir took her arm, and they went out into the street.

THE WIND AT BENI MIDAR

THE WIND AT BENI MIDAR

At Beni Midar there is a barracks. It has many rows of small buildings, whitewashed, and everything is in the middle of big rocks, on the side of the mountain behind the town. A quiet place when the wind is not blowing. A few Spanish still live in the houses along the road. They run the shops. But now the people in the streets are Moslems, mountain men with goats and sheep, or soldiers from the *cuartel* looking for wine. The Spanish sell wine to men they know. One Jew sells it to almost anybody. But there never is enough wine in the town for everybody who wants it. Beni Midar has only one street, that comes down out of the mountains, curves back and forth like a snake between the houses for a while, and goes on, back into the mountains. Sunday is a bad day, the one free time the soldiers have, when they can walk back and forth all day between the shops and the houses. A few Spaniards in black clothes go into the church at the hour when the Rhmara ride their donkeys out of the *souk*. Later the Spaniards come out of the church and go home. Nothing else happens because all the shops are shut. There is nothing the soldiers can buy.

Driss had been stationed for eight months in Beni Midar. Because the cabran in charge of his unit had been a neighbor of his in Tetuan, he was not unhappy. The cabran had a

71

friend with a motorcycle. Together they went each month to Tetuan. There the cabran always saw Driss's sister, who made a big bundle of food to send back to the barracks for him. She sent him chickens and cakes, cigarettes and figs, and always many hard-boiled eggs. He shared the eggs with two or three friends, and did not complain about being in Beni Midar.

Not even the brothels were open on Sunday. It was the day when everyone walked from one end of the town to the other, back and forth, many times. Sometimes Driss walked like this with his friends. Usually he took his gun and went down into the valley to hunt for hares. When he came back at twilight he stopped in a small café at the edge of town and had a glass of tea and a few pipes of kif. If it had not been the only café he would never have gone into it. Shameful things happened there. Several times he had seen men from the mountains get up from the mat and do dances that left blood on the floor. These men were Jilala, and no one thought of stopping them, not even Driss. They did not dance because they wanted to dance, and it was this that made him angry and ashamed. It seemed to him that the world should be made in such a way that a man is free to dance or not as he feels. A Jilali can do only what the music tells him to do. When the musicians, who are Jilala too, play the music that has the power, his eyes shut and he falls on the floor. And until the man has shown the proof and drunk his own blood, the musicians do not begin the music that will bring him back to the world. They should do something about it, Driss said to the other soldiers who went with him to the café, and they agreed.

The Wind at Beni Midar

He had talked about it with his cabran in the public garden. The cabran said that when all the children in the land were going to school every day there would be no more *djenoun*. Women would no longer be able to put spells on their husbands. And the Jilala and the Hamatcha and all the others would stop cutting their legs and arms and chests. Driss thought about this for a long time. He was glad to hear that the government knew about these bad things. "But if they know," he thought, "why don't they do something now? The day they get every one of the children in school I'll be lying beside Sidi Ali el Mandri." He was thinking of the cemetery at Bab Sebta in Tetuan. When he saw the cabran again he said: "If they can do something about it, they ought to do it now." The cabran did not seem interested. "Yes," he said.

When Driss got his permission and went home he told his father what the cabran had said. "You mean the government thinks it can kill all evil spirits?" his father cried.

"That's right. It can," said Driss. "It's going to."

His father was old and had no confidence in the young men who now ran the government. "It's impossible," he said. "They should let them alone. Leave them under their stones. Children have gone to school before, and how many were hurt by *djenoun*? But if the government begins to make trouble for them, you'll see what will happen. They'll go after the children first."

Driss had expected his father to speak this way, but when he heard the words he was ashamed. He did not answer. Some of his friends were without respect for God. They ate during Ramadan and argued with their fathers.

He was glad not to be like them. But he felt his father was wrong.

One hot summer Sunday when the sky was very blue Driss lay in bed late. The men who slept in his room at the barracks had gone out. He listened to the radio. "It would be good down in the valley on a day like this," he thought. He saw himself swimming in one of the big pools, and he thought of the hot sun on his back afterward. He got up and unlocked the cupboard to look for his gun. Even before he took it out he said, *"Yah latif!"* because he remembered that he had only one cartridge left, and it was Sunday. He slammed the cupboard door shut and got back into bed. The radio began to give the news. He sat up, spat as far out as he could from the bed, and turned it off. In the silence he heard many birds singing in the *safsaf* tree outside the window. He scratched his head. Then he got up and dressed. In the courtyard he saw Mehdi going toward the stairs. Mehdi was on his way to do sentry duty in the box outside the main gate.

"Khaï! Does four rials sound good to you?"

Medhi looked at him. "Is this number sixty, three, fifty-one?" This was the name of an Egyptian song that came over the radio nearly every day. The song ended with the word nothing. Nothing, nothing, sung over and over again.

Why not? As they walked along together, Driss moved closer, so that his thigh rubbed against Mehdi's.

"The price is ten, *khoya.*"

"With all its cartidges?"

"You want me to open it up and show you here?"

74

Mehdi's voice was angry. The words came out of the side of his mouth.

Driss said nothing. they came to the top of the stairs. Mehdi was walking fast. "You'll have to have it back here by seven," he said. "Do you want it?"

In his head Driss saw the long day in the empty town. "Yes," he said. "Stay there." He hurried back to the room, unlocked his cupboard, and took out his gun. From the shelf he pulled down his pipe, his kif, and a loaf of bread. He put his head outside the door. There was no one in the courtyard but Mehdi sitting on the wall at the other end. Then with the old gun in his hands he ran all the way to Mehdi. Mehdi took it and went down the stairs, leaving his own gun lying on the wall. Driss took up the gun, waited a moment, and followed him. When he went past the sentry box he heard Mehdi's voice say softly: "I need the ten at seven, *khoya.*"

Driss grunted. He knew how dark it was in there. No officer ever stuck his head inside the door on Sundays. Ten rials, he thought, and he's running no risk. He looked around at the goats among the rocks. The sun was hot, but the air smelled sweet, and he was happy to be walking down the side of the mountain. He pulled the visor of his cap further down over his eyes and began to whistle. Soon he came out in front of the town, below it on the other side of the valley. He could see the people on the benches in the park at the top of the cliff, small but clear and black. They were Spaniards and they were waiting for the bell of their church to begin to ring.

He got to the highest pool about the time the sun was overhead. When he lay on the rocks afterward eating his bread, the sun burned him. No animals will move before three, he thought. He put his trousers on and crawled into the shade of the oleander bushes to sleep. When he awoke the air was cooler. He smoked all the kif he had, and went walking through the valley. Sometimes he sang. He found no hares, and so he put small stones on the tops of the rocks and fired at them. Then he climbed back up the other side of the valley and followed the highway into the town.

He came to the café and went in. The musicians were playing and singing. The tea drinkers clapped their hands with the music. A soldier cried: "Driss! Sit down!" He sat with his friends and smoked some of their kif. Then he bought four rials' worth from the cutter who sat on the platform with the musicians, and went on smoking. "Nothing was moving in the valley today," he told them. "It was dead down there."

A man with a yellow turban on his head who sat nearby closed his eyes and fell against the man next to him. The others around him moved to a further part of the mat. The man toppled over and lay on the floor.

"Another one?" cried Driss. "They should stay in Djebel Habib. I can't look at him."

The man took a long time to get to his feet. His arms and legs had been captured by the drums, but his body was fighting, and he groaned. Driss tried to pay attention to him. He smoked his pipe and looked at his friends, pretending that no Jilali was in front of him. When the man pulled out his knife he could not pretend any longer. He watched the blood running into the man's eyes. It made a blank red curtain over each hole. The man opened his eyes wider, as if he wanted to see through the blood. The drums were loud.

Driss got up and paid the *qahouaji* for his tea. He said good-bye to the others and went out. The sun would soon go below the top of the mountains. Its light made him want to shut his eyes, because he had a lot of kif in his head. He walked through the town to the higher end and turned into a lane that led up into another valley. In this place there was no one. Cactuses grew high on each side of the lane, and the spiders had built a world of webs between their thorns. Because he walked fast, the kif began to boil in his head. Soon he was very hungry, but all the fruit had been picked from the cactuses along the lane. He came to a small farmhouse with a thatched roof. Behind it on the empty mountainside there were more cactuses still pink with hundreds of *hindiyats*. A dog in a shed beside the house began to bark. There was no sign of people. He stood still for a while and listened to the dog. Then he walked toward the cactus patch. He was sure no one was in the house. Many years ago his sister had shown him how to pick *hindiyats* without letting the needles get into the flesh of his hands. He laid his gun on the ground behind a low stone wall and began to gather the fruit. As he picked he saw in his head the two blind red holes of the Jilali's eyes, and under his breath he cursed all Jilala. When he had a great pile of fruit on the ground he sat down and began to eat, throwing the peels over his shoulder. As he ate he grew hungrier, and so he picked more. The picture he had in his head of the man's face shiny with blood slowly faded. He thought only of the *hindiyats* he was eating. It was almost dark there on the mountainside. He looked at his watch and jumped, because he remembered that Mehdi had to have his gun at seven o'clock. In the dim light he could not see the gun anywhere. He searched behind the wall, where he thought he had laid it, but he saw only stones and bushes.

"It's gone, *Allah istir*," he said. His heart pounded. He ran back to the lane and stood there a while. The dog barked without stopping.

It was dark before he reached the gate of the barracks. Another man was in the sentry box. The cabran was waiting for him in the room. The old gun Driss's father had given him lay on his bed.

"Do you know where Mehdi is?" the cabran asked him.

"No," said Driss.

"He's in the dark house, the son of a whore. And do you know why?"

Driss sat down on the bed. The cabran is my friend, he was thinking. "It's gone," he said, and told him how he had laid the gun on the ground, and a dog had been barking, and no one had come by, and still it had disappeared. "Maybe the dog was a *djinn*," he said when he had finished. He did not really believe the dog had anything to do with it, but he could not think of anything else to say then.

The cabran looked at him a long time and said nothing. He shook his head. "I thought you had some brains," he said at last. Then his face grew very angry, and he pulled Driss out into the courtyard and told a soldier to lock him up.

At ten o'clock that night he went to see Driss. He found him smoking his *sebsi* in the dark. The cell was full of kif smoke. "Garbage!" cried the cabran, and he took the pipe and the kif away from him. "Tell the truth," he said to Driss. "You sold the gun, didn't you?"

"On my mother's head, it's just as I told you! There was only the dog!"

The cabran could not make him say anything different. He slammed the door and went to the café in the town to have a glass of tea. He sat listening to the music, and he began to smoke the kif he had taken from Driss. If Driss was telling the truth, then it was only the kif in Driss's head that had made him lose the gun, and in that case there was a chance that it could be found.

The cabran had not smoked in a long time. As the kif filled his head he began to be hungry, and he remembered the times when he had been a boy smoking kif with his friends. Always they had gone to look for *hindiyats* afterward, because they tasted better than anything else and cost nothing. They always knew where there were some growing. "A *kouffa* full of good *hindiyats*," he thought. He shut his eyes and went on thinking.

The next mornng early the cabran went out and stood on a high rock behind the barracks, looking carefully all around the valley and the bare mountainside. Not far away he saw a lane with cactuses along it, and further up there was a whole forest of cactus. "There," he said to himself.

He walked among the rocks until he came to the lane, and he followed the lane to the farmhouse. The dog began to bark. A woman came to the doorway and looked at him.

He paid no attention to her, but went straight to the high cactuses on the hillside behind the house. There were many *hindiyats* still to be eaten, but the cabran did not eat any of them. He had no kif in his head and he was thinking only of the gun. Beside a stone wall there was a big pile of *hindiya* peelings. Someone had eaten a great many. Then he saw the sun shining on part of the gun's barrel under the peelings. "Hah!" he shouted, and he seized the gun and wiped it all over with his handkerchief. On his way back to the barracks he felt so happy that he decided to play a joke on Driss.

He hid the gun under his bed. With a glass of tea and a piece of bread in his hand he went to see Driss. He found him asleep on the floor in the dark.

"Daylight is here!" he shouted. He laughed and kicked Driss's foot to wake him up. Driss sat on the floor drinking the tea and the cabran stood in the doorway scratching his chin. He looked down at the floor, but not at Driss. After a time he said: "Last night you told me a dog was barking?"

Driss was certain the cabran was going to make fun of him. He was sorry he had mentioned the dog. "Yes," he said, not sounding sure.

"If it was the dog," the cabran went on, "I know how to get it back. You have to help me."

Driss looked up at him. He could not believe the cabran was being serious. Finally he said in a low voice: "I was joking when I said that. I had kif in my head."

The cabran was angry. "You think it's a joke to lose a gun that belongs to the Sultan? You did sell it! You haven't got kif in your head now. Maybe you can tell the truth." He stepped toward Driss, and Driss thought he was going to hit him. He stood up quickly. "I told you the truth," he said. "It was gone."

The cabran rubbed his chin and looked down at the floor again for a minute. "The next time a Jilali begins to dance in the café, we'll do it," he told him. He shut the door and left Driss alone.

Two days later the cabran came again into the dark house. He had another soldier with him. "Quick!" he told Driss. "There's one dancing now."

They went out into the courtyard and Driss blinked his eyes. "Listen," said the cabran. "When the Jilali is drinking his own blood he has power. What you have to do is ask him to make the *djinn* bring me the gun. I'm going to sit in my room and burn *djaoui*. That may help."

"I'll do it," said Driss. "But it won't do any good."

The other soldier took Driss to the café. The Jilali was a tall man from the mountains. He had already taken out his knife, and he was waving it in the air. The soldier made Driss sit down near the musicians, and then he waited until the man began to lick the blood from his arms. Then, because he thought he might be sick if he watched any longer, Driss raised his right arm toward the Jilali and said in a low voice, "In the name of Allah, *khoya*, make the *djinn* that stole Mehdi's gun take it now to Aziz the cabran." The Jilali seemed to be staring at him, but Driss could not be sure whether he had heard his words or not.

The soldier took him back to the barracks. The cabran was sitting under a plum tree beside the kitchen door. He told the soldier to go away and jumped up. "Come," he said, and he led Driss to the room. The air was blue with the smoke of the *djaoui* he had been burning. He pointed to the middle of the floor. "Look!" he cried. A gun was lying there. Driss ran and picked it up. After he had looked at it carefully, he said: "It's the gun." And his voice was full of fear. The cabran could see that Driss had not been sure the thing was possible, but that now he no longer had any doubt.

The cabran was happy to have fooled him so easily. He laughed. "You see, it worked," he said. "It's lucky for you Mehdi's going to be in the dark house for another week."

Driss did not answer. He felt even worse than when he had been watching the Jilali slicing the flesh of his arms.

That night he lay in bed worrying. It was the first time he had had anything to do with a *djinn* or *affrit*. Now he had entered into their world. It was a dangerous world and he did not trust the cabran any longer. "What am I going to do?" he thought. The men all around him were sleeping, but he could not close his eyes. Soon he got up and stepped outside. The leaves of the *safsaf* tree were hissing in the wind. On the other side of the courtyard there was light in one of the windows. Some of the officers were talking there. He walked slowly around the garden in the middle and looked up at the sky, thinking of how different his life was going to be now. As he came near the lighted window he heard a great burst of laughter. The cabran was telling a story. Driss stopped walking and listened.

"And he said to the Jalili: 'Please, sidi, would you ask the dog that stole my gun—' "

The men laughed again, and the sound covered the cabran's voice.

He went quickly back and got into bed. If they knew he had heard the cabran's story they would laugh even more. He lay in the bed thinking, and he felt poison come into his heart. It was the cabran's fault that the *djinn* had been called, and now in front of his superior officers he was pretending that he had had nothing to do with it. Later the cabran came in and went to bed, and it was quiet in the courtyard, but Driss lay thinking for a long time before he went to sleep.

In the days that came after that, the cabran was friendly again, but Driss did not want to see him smile. He thought with hatred: "In his head I'm afraid of him now because he knows how to call a *djinn*. He jokes with me now because he has power."

He could not laugh or be happy when the cabran was nearby. Each night he lay awake for a long time after the others had gone to sleep. He listened to the wind moving the hard leaves of the *safsaf* tree, and he thought only of how he could break the cabran's power.

When Mehdi came out of the dark house he spoke against the cabran. Driss paid him his ten rials. "A lot of money for ten days in the dark house," Mehdi grumbled, and he looked at the bill in his hand. Driss pretended not to understand. "He's a son of a whore," he said.

Mehdi snorted. "And you have the head of a needle," he said. "It all came from you. The wind blows kif out of your ears!"

"You think I wasn't in the dark house too?" cried Driss. But he could not tell Mehdi about the Jilali and the dog. "He's a son of a whore," he said again.

A Hundred Camels in the Courtyard

Mehdi's eyes grew narrow and stiff. "I'll do his work for him. He'll think he's in the dark house himself when I finish."

Mehdi went on his way. Driss stood watching him go.

The next Sunday Driss got up early and walked into Beni Midar. The *souk* was full of rows of mountain people in white clothes. He walked in among the donkeys and climbed the steps to the stalls. There he went to see an old man who sold incense and herbs. People called him El Fqih. He sat down in front of El Fqih and said: "I want something for a son of a whore."

El Fqih looked at him angrily. "A sin!" He raised his forefinger and shook it back and forth. "Sins are not my work." Driss did not say anything. El Fqih spoke more quietly now. "To balance that, it is said that each trouble in the world has its remedy. There are cheap remedies and remedies that cost a lot of money." He stopped.

Driss waited. "How much is this one?" he asked him. The old man was not pleased because he wanted to talk longer. But he said: "I'll give you a name for five rials." He looked sternly at Driss, leaned forward and whispered a name in his ear. "In the alley behind the sawmill," he said aloud. "The blue tin shack with the canebrake in back of it." Driss paid him and ran down the steps.

He found the house. The old woman stood in the doorway with a checkered tablecloth over her head. Her eyes had turned white like milk. They looked to Driss like the eyes of an old dog. He said: "You're Anisa?"

"Come into the house," she told him. It was almost dark inside. He told her he wanted something to break the power of a son of a whore. "Give me ten rials now," she said. "Come back at sunset with another ten. It will be ready."

After the midday meal he went out into the courtyard. He met Mehdi and asked him to go with him to the café in Beni Midar. They walked through the town in the hot afternoon sun. It was still early when they got to the café, and there was plenty of space on the mats. They sat in a dark corner. Driss took out his kif and his *sebsi* and they smoked. When the musicians began to play, Mehdi said: "The circus is back!" But Driss did not want to talk about the Jilala. He talked about the cabran. He gave the pipe many times to Mehdi, and he watched Mehdi growing more angry with the cabran as he smoked. He was not surprised when Mehdi cried: "I'll finish it tonight!"

"No, *khoya,*" said Driss. "You don't know. He's gone way up. He's a friend of all the officers now. They bring him bottles of wine."

"He'll come down," Mehdi said. "Before dinner tonight. In the courtyard. You be there and watch it."

Driss handed him the pipe and paid for the tea. He left Mehdi there and went into the street to walk up and down because he did not want to sit still any longer. When the sky was red behind the mountain he went to the alley by the sawmill. The old woman was in the doorway.

"Come in," she said as before. When they were inside the room she handed him a paper sack. "He has to take all of it," she said. She took the money and pulled at his sleeve. "I never saw you," she said. "Good-bye."

Driss went to his room and listened to the radio. When dinner time came he stood inside the doorway looking out into the courtyard. In the shadows at the other end he thought he could see Mehdi, but he was not sure. There were many soldiers walking around in the courtyard, waiting for dinner. Soon there was shouting near the top of the steps. the soldiers began to run toward the other end of the courtyard. Driss looked from the doorway and saw only the running soldiers. He called to the men in the room. "Something's happening!" They all ran out. Then with the paper of powder in his hand he went back into the room to the cabran's bed and lifted up the bottle of wine one of the offices had given the cabran the day before. It was almost full. He pulled out the cork and let the powder slide into the bottle. He shook the bottle and put the cork back. There was still shouting in the courtyard. He ran out. When he got near the crowd, he saw Mehdi being dragged along the round by three soldiers. He was kicking. The cabran sat on the wall with his head down, holding his arm. There was blood all over his face and shirt.

It was almost a half hour before the cabran came to eat his dinner. His face was covered with bruises and his arm was bandaged and hung in a sling. Mehdi had cut it with his knife at the last minute whent he soldiers had begun to pull them apart. The cabran did not speak much, and the men did not try to talk with him. He sat on his bed and ate. While he was eating he drank all the wine in the bottle.

That night the cabran moaned in his sleep. A dry wind between the mountains. It made a great noise in the *safsaf* tree outside the window. The air roared and the leaves rattled, but Driss still heard the cabran's voice crying. In the morning the doctor came to look at him. The cabran's eyes were open but he could not see. And his mouth was open but he could not speak. They carried him out of the room where the soldiers lived and put him somewhere else. "Maybe the power is broken now," thought Driss.

A few days later a truck came to the barracks, and he saw two men carrying the cabran on a stretcher to the truck. Then he was sure that the cabran's soul had been torn out of his body and that the power was truly broken. In his head he made a prayer of thanks to Allah. He stood with some other soldiers on a rock above the barracks watching the truck grow smaller as it moved down the mountain.

"It's bad for me," he told a man who stood nearby. "He always brought me food from home." The soldier shook his head.

GLOSSARY

AOUADAS. Large transversal flutes
BERRADA. A water jug
CHOUWAL. The lunar month following Ramadan
CHQAF. The bowl of the kif pipe
CUARTEL. Barracks
DJELLABA. A cloak with hood
DJINN. A spirit, generally malicious
EN NOUAR. Flowers (popularly syphilis)
FJER. The call to prayer an hour before dawn
HAIK. The traditional female outer garment
HAOUMA. A neighborhood
HAMATCHA. A religious brotherhood
HINDIYATS. Prickly pears
JDUQ JMEL. A plant resembling jimson weed
JEHENNEM. Hell
JILALA. A religious brotherhood
JOYTEYA. A flea market
KHOYA. Conversational term for brother
KOUFFA. A large sack or bag
MCID. A Koranic primary school
MEDINA. A city (in Morocco used to designate the
    non-European quarter)
MELLAH. The Jewish quarter of a town
MENDOUB. In international Tangier, the
    sultan's representative
MIJMAH. A brazier
MKIYIF. Affected by having smoked kif
MOTTOUI. A kif pouch

MUEZZIN. The man who makes the call to prayer
from a minaret

NAQOUS. A circular metal object (often a brake drum)
used as percussion

NCHAIOUI. A man who devotes all his time to smoking kif

QAHOUAJI. A man who prepares or serves tea in a cafe

SALA. A living room

SAFSAF. A eucalyptus tree

SEBSI. The stem of a kif pipe

SEGUIA. An irrigation channel

SOUK. A market

YEHOUDIA. A Jewish woman

ALSO AVAILABLE FROM
CITY LIGHTS BOOKS

M'HASHISH
*by Mohammed Mrabet, translated from the Moghrebi
by Paul Bowles*
A City Lights classic: ten unforgettable tales by the
celebrated Moroccan storyteller.
"One of the world's more remarkable literary
collaborations."—*The Village Voice*
ISBN 0-87286-034-5 $3.95

THE LEMON
*by Mohammed Mrabet, translated from the Moghrebi
by Paul Bowles*
The adventures of Abdeslam, a precocious twelve-year old
Moroccan boy who runs away from his home in the Rif
Mountains in North Africa to Tangier.
"A surprisingly effective book."—*The New Yorker*
"The naturalness of the telling is the sort that artists
like Hemingway have sweated blood
to attain."—*The Oxford Mail*
ISBN 0-87286-181-3 $6.95

THE OBLIVION SEEKERS
*by Isabelle Eberhardt, translated from the French
by Paul Bowles*
Tender and illuminating glimpses of North Africa by a
legendary vagabond scholar.
"One of the strangest human documents that a woman has
given to the world."—Cecily Mackworth
ISBN 0-87286-082-5 $5.95

LOVE WITH A FEW HAIRS

by Mohammed Mrabet, translated from the Moghrebi
by Paul Bowles

Mohammed Mrabet's formidable first novel about a young
man coming of age in contemporary Morocco - a lively tale
of innocence, experience and obsession.
"The absolute simplicity of the narrative
allies the novel with some of the most sophisticated
new fiction."—*Saturday Review of Literature*
ISBN 0-87286-192-9 $6.95

THE BEGGAR'S KNIFE

by Rodgrigo Rey Rosa, translated from the Spanish
by Paul Bowles

From one of Guatemala's finest young writers, a collection of
riveting stories - at once brutal and intensely lyrical.
"A marvel of poetic efficiency and power."
—*San Francisco Chronicle*
ISBN 0-87286-166-X $12.95
ISBN 0-87286-164-3 (pbk.) $5.95

FOR BREAD ALONE

by Mohamed Choukri, translated from the Arabic
by Paul Bowles

The extraordinary autobiography of a young Moroccan
growing up in an environment of extreme poverty
and deprivation.
"A true document of human desperation, shattering in
its impact."—Tennessee Williams
ISBN 0-87286-196-1 (pbk.) $6.95